GREEN WILMA

GREEN WILMA

Tedd Arnold

A Puffin Pied Piper

For Imogene,
Wilma, and
Green Dog

PUFFIN BOOKS
Published by the Penguin Group
Penguin Putnam Inc., 375 Hudson Street, New York, New York 10014, U.S.A.
Penguin Books Ltd, 27 Wrights Lane, London W8 5TZ, England
Penguin Books Australia Ltd, Ringwood, Victoria, Australia
Penguin Books Canada Ltd, 10 Alcorn Avenue, Toronto, Ontario, Canada M4V 3B2
Penguin Books (N.Z.) Ltd, 182-190 Wairau Road, Auckland 10, New Zealand

Penguin Books Ltd, Registered Offices: Harmondsworth, Middlesex, England

First published in the United States of America by Dial Books for Young Readers,
a division of Penguin Books USA Inc., 1993
Published in Puffin Books, 1998

15 17 19 20 18 16

THE LIBRARY OF CONGRESS HAS CATALOGED THE DIAL EDITION AS FOLLOWS:
Arnold, Tedd.
Green Wilma / by Tedd Arnold.—1st ed. p. cm.
Summary: Waking up with a frog-like appearance, Wilma proves disruptive at school as
she searches for some tasty flies.
ISBN 0-8037-1313-4—ISBN 0-8037-1314-2 (lib.)
[1. Frogs—Fiction. 2. Schools—Fiction. 3. Stories in rhyme.] I. Title.
PZ8.3.A647GR 1993 [E]—dc20 91-31501 CIP AC

Puffin Books ISBN 978-0-14-056362-7

Printed in the United States of America

*The art for this book was created using watercolor paint and colored pencil. It was then
color-separated and reproduced as red, blue, yellow, and black halftones.*

One morning Wilma woke up green, and
much to her surprise

She sat up on her bed and croaked and
started eating flies.

She washed, she dressed, she combed her hair,
she quickly made her bed.

She hopped down to the breakfast table.
"Pass the bugs," she said.

"Green children should not go to school,"
she heard her mother fuss.

But out the window Wilma jumped and
rode off on the bus.

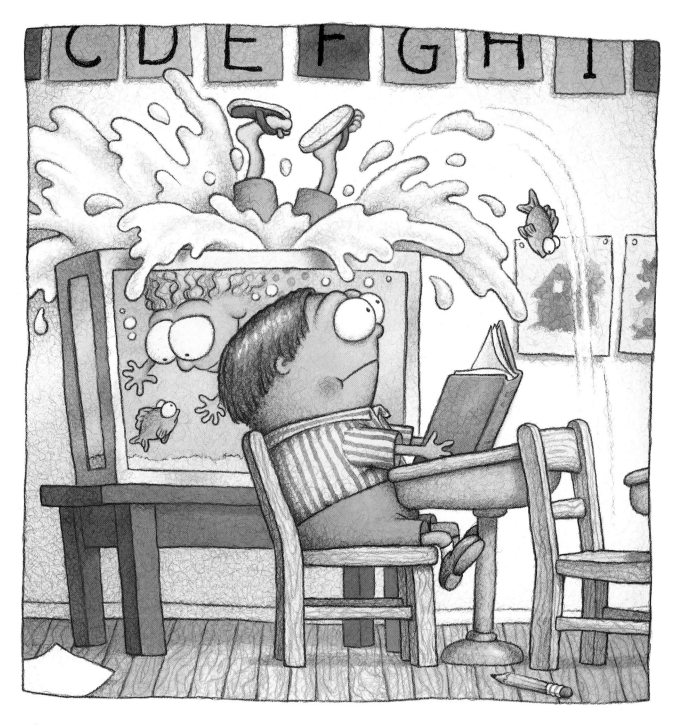

In class Green Wilma tried but simply
couldn't keep her seat.

In gym while playing dodgeball Wilma
never could be beat.

In art the kids thought being green was
absolutely great!

But Teacher said, "The green must be from
something that she ate."

At story time poor Wilma felt so
hungry she could cry.

And then she saw on Teacher's nose a
tasty little fly.

She chased it all around the room and
up and down the hall,

And through the lunchroom (that's the place that
flies love best of all).

The principal yelled, "Stop her! She should
know we have a rule

That children aren't allowed to munch on
flies while they're in school."

Then out the door Green Wilma hopped,
into the hills beyond,

And finally she caught that fly
up over Miller's Pond.

Wilma landed in the water
with a noisy splash,

She met a very hungry fish.

and woke up in a flash.

Then she recalled the words they teach to
every little frog,

"When you dream, be careful that you
don't fall off the log."